DATE DUE

JUL.05.1995		
FEB.08.1996		
FEB.20.1996		
MAR12.1996		
APR.24.1996		
MAY15.1995		
JUN.05.1996		
AUG 16.1997		
JUN.24.1999		
JAN.14.2000		
MAR18.2000		

Inc. 38-293

It's OK to Be You

A Frank and Funny Guide to Growing Up

Claire Patterson
Illustrated by Lindsay Quilter

TRICYCLE PRESS
Berkeley, California

It's OK to Be You

A Kirsty Melville book

TRICYCLE PRESS
P O Box 7123
Berkeley, California 94707

Originally published in different form in the United States by Meadowbrook Press.

Library of Congress Cataloging-in-Publication Date

Patterson, Claire.
        It's OK to be you : a frank and funny guide to growing up / Claire Patterson : illustrated by Lindsay Quilter. — Rev. ed.
        p. cm.
        This ed. is a revision of the previous American ed. published by Meadowbrook Press, 1988 entitled: Almost grown up.
        ISBN 1-883672-16-3
        1. Puberty—Juvenile literature. 2. Sex instruction for children. 3. Teenagers—Health and hygiene—Juvenile literature.
4. Emotions—Juvenile literature. [1. Puberty. 2. Sex instruction for children. 3. Emotions.] I. Quilter, Lindsay Ill. II. Patterson, Claire. Almost grown up. III. Title. IV. Title: It's okay to be you!
        QP84.4.P37 1994
        612.6'61—dc20   94-17791
                                                                              CIP
                                                                              AC

First published in 1988 by Shoal Bay Press, Christchurch, New Zealand
First Tricycle Press printing, 1994
Manufactured in Hong Kong
1 2 3 4 5 6 — 98 97 96 95 94

Contents

About This Book

This book is about you. It's about your body and your feelings and the changes in you when you start becoming an adult.

A lot of grown-ups don't talk much to kids about these things. They might have forgotten what it's like to be your age, or they might feel too embarrassed to bring the subject up. Sometimes adults don't think they know enough themselves or think you can work things out on your own — like they did perhaps?

Sometimes your friends don't talk much either. They might feel embarrassed about what's happening to them, they might be unsure about how other people will react, or they have been taught that it's 'rude' to talk about such things. They might pretend they know everything there is to know, or have some pretty weird ideas that aren't going to be much use to anyone.

One thing's for sure: knowing what's going on and what to expect makes things a whole lot easier. Having accurate information helps you to understand the changes you will go through and gives you somewhere to start if you want to ask questions.

It's always nice to have someone to talk things over with — maybe sharing this book together will get you started.

Introducing ...

STEVIE
(12 years old)

Pretends he knows it all (but he doesn't of course).

MIKE-O
(11 years old)

Unsure of himself and often feels inadequate. He tries to be friendly and nice.

"HORSE"
(12 years old)

Has decided she's a horse, not a girl. A vegetarian. Gorges on chocolate when-ever she can.

"ICECREAM"
(10 years old)

Very worried about the size of his ears.

MELANIE-MORGAN
(11 Years old)

GRAM
(63 years old)

MUNCHKIN
(108 years old)

Wise and confident. She knows a lot because she spends a lot of time talking to Gram.

Melanie-Morgan's grandmother — the sort of grandmother a lot of kids would like to have.

Nothing surprises him — he has seen it all before!

You and Your Body

Feeling Good

Bodies can be wonderful. Think of all the things you can do and feel with your body. Here are some of the things people have said make them feel good.

climbing trees running swimming
lying still and listening to sounds
dancing doing handstands
brushing my hair making faces
my smell having a bath
sleeping in waking up
stretching yawning eating
laughing burping farting
listening to music lying in the sun
rubbing on suntan oil
picking my nose jumping in puddles
working hard getting dressed up
staying in my pyjamas all day

You probably have some favorite things of your own to add to the list.

Looking Different

Think of all the ways you can look different from your friends: different sizes and shapes, different skin color, hair, faces, noses and ears. Even the parts you may not pay much attention to, like hands and feet and eyebrows, are different. Think what it would be like if everyone looked the same.

I PROBABLY HAVE THE BIGGEST EARS IN THE WORLD °°°°

WHEN I WAS SMALL, MY FATHER USED TO CALL ME "RABBiT"!

BUT SINCE I STARTED WEARING THIS CONE ON MY NOSE°°°

°°° NOBODY EVEN **NOTICES** MY EARS! NOBODY EVER CALLS ME "RABBiT" ANYMORE!°°

HEY °iCECREAM! STRAWBERRY °iCECREAM! HA HA HA HA **HA**

SIGH°°° OF COURSE, NOTHING IS ABSOLUTELY **PERFECT**°°°

12

Being Different Is Normal

One reason people look different is because everyone has different genes. Genes are found in the cells of your body and are responsible for whether you have black, brown or white skin, have straight or curly hair, brown or blue eyes, freckles, or dimples, or any of the things that make you a special person.

You inherit a mixture of genes from your parents. That's why you often look a bit like your mother and a bit like your father.

Another reason you can look different is that people grow up differently. People eat different food, get different kinds of exercise and do different work. Sometimes the air people breathe is clean and sometimes it is polluted. Diseases or accidents can change the way you look. All the things around you, your environment, help make you the sort of person you are.

A third reason is that people grow up feeling different things. Everyone has things that bother them from time to time. If you have lots to worry about in your life, lots to feel tense about and to feel scared about, you may start to look worried, anxious or scared all the time.

Worrying about looking different

Even if they know why they look different, lots of people still worry about it. Here are some things that people have said bother them:

my pointy nose   having too many freckles
being really thin   wearing glasses
being too short   being too tall   pimples
being flat-chested   feeling fat
having to wear a bra   wearing braces
having skinny arms and no muscles
I worry that I smell funny
having red hair   the size of my bottom

Perhaps there are things you could add to this list.

13

It helps to realize that while you're worrying away about some part of you that's not the way you'd like it to be, most other people probably haven't even noticed it.

Have you ever thought about why people don't feel OK about themselves and the way they look?

Things That Can Affect the Way You Feel About Yourself

Things people say

Sometimes things people say to you can make you feel as if there is something wrong with the way you look, when there is really nothing wrong at all.

Without even meaning to be unkind someone might make a comment like:

'Your eyes are really close together.'

or

'Your penis is really small, isn't it?'

Sometimes the person means to be cruel:

'Ha, ha you're fat!'

Teasing and thoughtless remarks can make you feel really embarrassed, and self-conscious. But remember that people who tease unkindly are often trying to take attention off something that they are worried or embarrassed about.

Other people's ideas about what you should look like

You can feel unsure about yourself if you think you don't fit in with other people's ideas about what looks 'good'. Lots of these ideas come from how people are portrayed in magazines, advertisements, comics and movies and on TV.

The women are often shaped like Barbie dolls — thick hair, long legs, tiny bottoms, breasts poked out, perfect teeth and skinny.

The men are tough guys with muscle-bound chests, tight stomachs and square jaws, and they are in control.

Hardly anyone ever has pimples, freckles, uneven teeth or knobbly knees; no one ever gets hot and bothered or looks the least bit unsure about life — unless they are there to be laughed at, used to show you how superior the hero is by comparison, or to sell you something to 'fix you up.'

15

The trouble with seeing all these 'perfect' people (they are called **stereotypes**) every time you turn on the television or open a magazine is that you can end up believing that unless you look and act like them you aren't going to be a successful or popular person.

Because of all this lots of kids try to change or hide the way they are by dieting, weight-lifting, acting 'cool' or buying the products advertised. Doing these things might boost confidence a bit, but the opposite often happens. If often makes people even more worried about themselves and the way they look.

Even if you don't care about looking like a stereotype, other people may want you to conform to one.

'Mom hassles me all the time about doing something about my clothes, my hair, my pimples, my big butt. It feels like she worries more about what other people think than how I feel.'

It can be hard to feel OK about the way you are when other people are trying to make you change. They might even think they are helping you become popular or more attractive, but it can make you feel the opposite.

The truth is that, in real life, learning to feel OK about how you look is the first step to being confident.

Feeling OK About How You Look

Feeling OK about how you look has to do with:

— enjoying your body;
— understanding that everyone is different;
— learning to be yourself and liking yourself just the way you are;
— learning to stand up for yourself.

Another part of feeling good about yourself is feeling comfortable about your whole body and understanding how your body works.

No Clothes

There are parts of our bodies that are covered up most of the time, so that even if you know how you look without clothes, you might not be familiar with how others look.

If nobody ever wore clothes you would probably treat the parts of bodies you don't usually see the same way you treat the parts you do usually see. But because you don't usually get to see what other people's bodies look like, it is natural to be curious.

Different people have different attitudes toward being naked. In some families, for instance, the adults and the kids feel relaxed about walking around with no clothes on. They might take baths together and they don't mind other people seeing them getting dressed or undressed.

Some families, on the other hand, like to have more privacy. They like to lock the bathroom or the lavatory door, and never appear out of the bedroom unless they are fully dressed.

The way people around you feel can affect the way you feel about your own body. It can also have an effect on how comfortable you feel about talking about your body.

If a person starts to feel uncomfortable in front of others it is common to try all sorts of things to avoid being embarrassed ...

19

20

... It would be easier if everyone were straightforward and could feel relaxed and comfortable with one another.

Talking About Your Body

Some people are brought up to think that it is not 'nice' to talk about some parts of their bodies. These people can get into tangles when they do need to talk.

TEE HEE

TEE HEE

WE TALKED about "DOWN THERE"...
"IT"...
"YOU KNOW WHERE"...
aND
"PRIVATE PARTS"

TEE HEE HEE

They use vague words like 'down there,' 'you know what' or 'private parts' or they invent names like 'tool,' 'thing,' 'the family jewels,' or 'pecker.' This makes it hard to know what they are talking about.

It's not just the way you are brought up that can affect how easy it is to talk about your body. At school other kids giggle about things they think are 'nasty,' or 'naughty,' or 'dirty.' When this happens it becomes harder to talk to your friends in a straightforward way and makes it easy to pick up a lot of wrong information.

Knowing the right words to use — the real names for parts of your body — will make talking about them much easier and more straightforward.

Your Body, Inside and Out

Even though everyone looks different, our bodies all function the same way. Inside our bodies we all have bones, a heart, lungs, kidneys, a liver, and other important organs that keep us alive.

You can't see what's inside you, but you can feel some things as they are working.

If you put your hand over your heart you can feel it pumping blood around your body.

If you put your hand just below your ribs and breathe in, you can feel your diaphragm moving out, drawing air into your lungs.

Sometimes what's going on in your body tells you something you need to know.

— If your body needs food you have an empty feeling and your stomach rumbles.
— If your body needs sleep you feel like stretching and yawning, which helps your body to relax so that you can sleep.

— If your body needs to empty out you feel pressure on your bowel or bladder which makes you want to go to the toilet.

In most ways men and women, boys and girls, are the same. But there are some differences. The most obvious one you can see is that boys and girls have different genitals. A boy's penis and testicles are part of his genitals and a girl's vagina and labia are part of hers. Let's take a closer look.

GIRL'S GENITALS
FROM THE OUTSIDE...

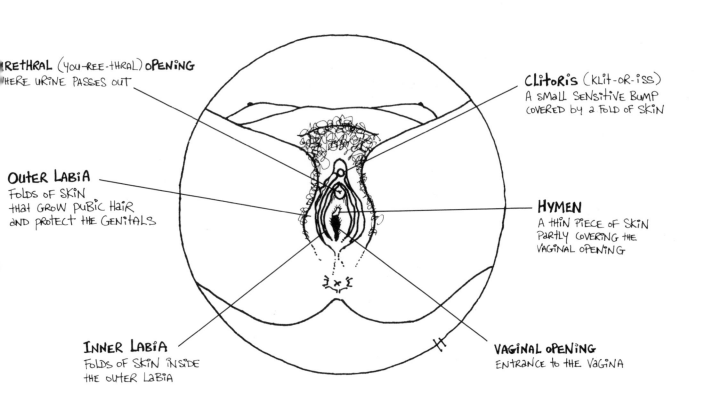

URETHRAL (YOU-REE-THRAL) **OPENING**
WHERE URINE PASSES OUT

CLITORIS (KLIT-OR-ISS)
A SMALL SENSITIVE BUMP
COVERED BY A FOLD OF SKIN

OUTER LABIA
FOLDS OF SKIN
THAT GROW PUBIC HAIR
AND PROTECT THE GENITALS

HYMEN
A THIN PIECE OF SKIN
PARTLY COVERING THE
VAGINAL OPENING

INNER LABIA
FOLDS OF SKIN INSIDE
THE OUTER LABIA

VAGINAL OPENING
ENTRANCE TO THE VAGINA

BOY'S GENITALS
FROM THE OUTSIDE...

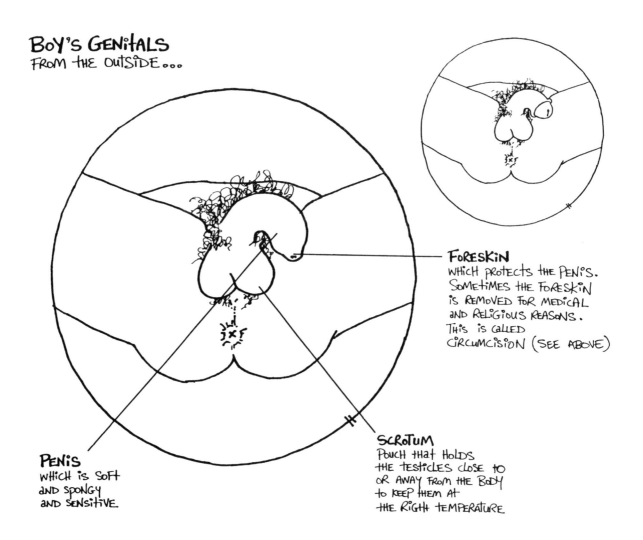

FORESKIN
WHICH PROTECTS THE PENIS. SOMETIMES THE FORESKIN IS REMOVED FOR MEDICAL AND RELIGIOUS REASONS. THIS IS CALLED CIRCUMCISION (SEE ABOVE)

PENIS
WHICH IS SOFT AND SPONGY AND SENSITIVE.

SCROTUM
POUCH THAT HOLDS THE TESTICLES CLOSE TO OR AWAY FROM THE BODY TO KEEP THEM AT THE RIGHT TEMPERATURE

24

Why Men and Women Are Different

The differences in men and women have to do with making babies (reproduction). A baby is started when a sperm from a man joins with (fertilizes) an egg (ovum) from a woman. This happens as a result of sexual intercourse.

Sexual intercourse is also known as making love, because it is a very warm, intimate and nice thing for two people to do together. Usually, the man and woman lie together, cuddling, stroking and kissing one another. This gives them pleasurable feelings which get stronger and make them want to get closer and closer together.

There are changes in their bodies as they become sexually excited. The man's penis becomes erect and the woman's vagina becomes more slippery. This makes it easier for the woman and man to guide his penis inside her vagina.

Cuddling close together and moving their hips around makes his penis move back and forth and around inside her vagina. The pleasurable feelings caused by this movement build up until the man ejaculates sperm or 'comes.'

Millions of tiny sperm spurt out of his penis into the woman's vagina. They are like microscopic 'tadpoles' which swim into her uterus and her oviducts. If there is an ovum in the oviduct, it takes just one sperm to fertilize it.

The ovum and sperm unite (this is known as conception) and together move into the uterus. Nine months later they will have developed and grown into a fully formed human baby.

When people make love they may each have an orgasm, which is when their intense and powerful feelings reach a peak and then ebb away leaving them both feeling warm and relaxed and close. Since people usually choose to make love for pleasure rather than to start a baby, they will use **birth control** to prevent this from happening. (This is also called family planning or contraception. You can find out about birth control from family planning clinics.)

As a child your reproductive organs are not fully developed. The time when your body changes physically from being that of a child to being that of an adult is called puberty. This is when your reproductive organs start to work like an adult's and when you start to look, think and feel in new and different ways.

Growing and Changing

The changes during puberty are gradual. You won't wake up one morning and discover you have become an adult overnight.

Everyone starts changing at a different age — usually any time between the ages of 9 or 16. Because everyone grows at a different rate you may find that some kids look much older while others look much younger than you. Girls tend to start changing and growing earlier than boys and often the girls in a class look much older than the boys.

As you grow, it can take time to get used to your longer arms and legs and your new body shape. You may find you are always banging into things and hurting yourself, but this will pass with time.

The signal that it is time for you to become an adult comes from hormones, which are chemical 'messengers' secreted from different glands in your body.

These hormones will also affect how you feel and think. It can take a while for your body, your feelings and your thoughts to catch up with one another.

Here are some of the changes you will notice in yourself and in your friends.

Longer arms and legs

Your legs usually get longer first, so you will probably start growing out of your jeans or skirts before you grow out of your shirts and sweaters. Your feet will grow bigger.

MELANIE-MORGAN, MY LOVE... Most OF ME THINKS THIS IS A WONDERFUL IDEA — But MY KNEES BOTH Say YOU'RE GETTING Too BiG!

Body shape

Both boys and girls continue to grow stronger. Girls develop more fatty tissue, particularly around their hips, which become broader. Boys will develop broader shoulders and a bigger chest than before. Boys and girls start to look quite different in shape from one another.

More sweat

Your sweat glands start working more and your smell changes.

More skin oil

Your skin gets oilier so that you may start getting pimples on your face, back or chest.

More hair

Some people are more hairy than others. At puberty many kids find that their hair grows thicker and darker on their legs and arms. It also grows under the arms and around the genitals. Pubic hair is soft at first but later it becomes coarser and curly. Boys often start to grow hair on their faces and on their chests.

Bigger voice

Both girls' and boys' voices deepen. Boys' voices can 'break' which means they sometimes change from high to low at unexpected moments. This settles down after a few months.

27

Breasts

Girls start to grow breasts and their nipples change in shape and color. Boys may notice a change in their nipples too, and sometimes they feel very tender.

Bigger genitals

A boy's penis and testicles will grow much larger; a girl's labia will grow larger too.

Feeling OK About all the Changes

Some kids worry about whether many of the changes they are experiencing are normal.

— One of my breasts is bigger than the other one. Am I normal?
— My penis goes to one side and Tony's is straight. Am I normal?
— I've got pubic hairs on the tops of my legs. Am I normal?
— My penis is much smaller than all the other boys'. Am I normal?

The answer to all these questions is yes. Remember what we said earlier? Being different is normal. If you talk to other kids your age, or ask a grown-up how it was for them, you'll discover that most people have felt worried or embarrassed or self-conscious at some time during puberty. Asking questions and sharing your feelings will help you understand and feel better about all the changes you experience at this time.

Changes Inside Your Body

Along with all the changes on the outside there are changes on the inside which you can't see but which will be responsible for new experiences. Boys start to produce sperm and girls' ova (eggs) begin to ripen. The outward signs of these things happening is that girls start to have periods and boys start to have ejaculations.

OMiGOODNESS! THERE'S **RED** STUFF ON MY PANTS!

...AND it's NOT STRAWBERRY **JAM**!

It's **BLOOD**! HELP! WHAT DO I DO? WHAT DO I DO?

It's ALL **RIGHT**, HORSE! YOU'RE MENSTRUATING...

WHAT's **THAT**?

I THINK it MEANS YOU CAN HAVE a BABY. OR THAT YOU'RE **NOT** GOING TO HAVE a BABY

...OR BOTH...

?!

LET'S ASK **GRAM**...!

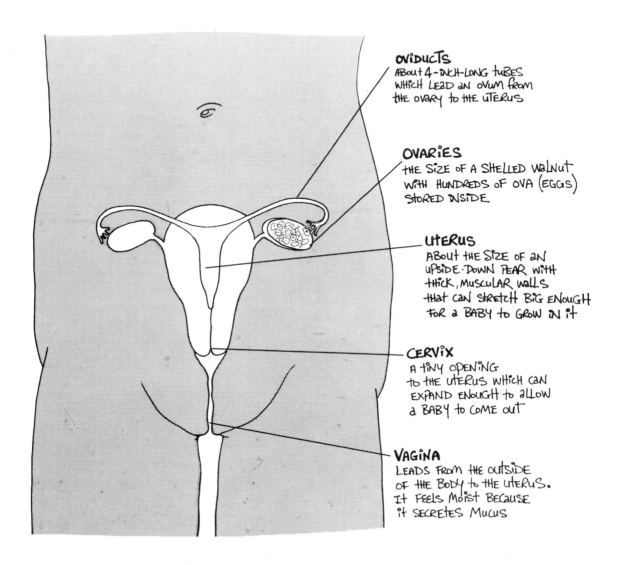

OVIDUCTS
ABOUT 4-INCH-LONG TUBES WHICH LEAD AN OVUM FROM THE OVARY TO THE UTERUS

OVARIES
THE SIZE OF A SHELLED WALNUT WITH HUNDREDS OF OVA (EGGS) STORED INSIDE

UTERUS
ABOUT THE SIZE OF AN UPSIDE-DOWN PEAR WITH THICK, MUSCULAR WALLS THAT CAN STRETCH BIG ENOUGH FOR A BABY TO GROW IN IT

CERVIX
A TINY OPENING TO THE UTERUS WHICH CAN EXPAND ENOUGH TO ALLOW A BABY TO COME OUT

VAGINA
LEADS FROM THE OUTSIDE OF THE BODY TO THE UTERUS. IT FEELS MOIST BECAUSE IT SECRETES MUCUS

Girls: Getting Your Period

When you are born you have thousands of immature ova (or eggs) in your ovaries. At puberty these eggs begin to ripen. This is the beginning of your **menstrual cycle**.

One ovum is released from one of your ovaries at regular intervals (usually once every 21 to 45 days). The ovum is wafted into the oviduct by tiny hairs at the entrance. It is moved along the oviduct by the muscular walls which tighten and relax until finally it reaches your uterus. In the meantime, the inside lining of your uterus has been preparing for the egg's arrival by becoming thick and spongy and full of tiny blood vessels.

If the ova has become fertilized it will implant itself in the lining of the uterus and slowly grow into a baby. If the ova has not been fertilized (which is usual) the special protective lining is not needed and it breaks away from the wall of your uterus. This mixture of blood and tissue and mucus then trickles out of your uterus, into the vagina to the outside. This is called having your period or **menstruation**.

The whole cycle then starts again. Another ova ripens and your uterus prepares a new lining in case it is fertilized.

The blood, tissue and mucus that come out when you are having a period looks red and oozy. The first part of the flow is usually bright red because the blood is new. Toward the end of your period it is a darker red because the blood is older. Sometimes you will see soft, lumpy clots of blood.

Here are some questions girls and boys often ask about periods.

When do you get your first period?

This is different for every girl, but you could probably expect to get your first period one to two years after your breasts start to develop or about a year after you grow pubic hair. You will probably be between nine and fifteen years old.

How often does it come?

A whole cycle, from the beginning of one period to the beginning of the next, can take anywhere from 21 to 45 days. Some girls have exactly the same number of days from the start of one period to the beginning of the next, which makes it easy to know when their next one is due.

Other girls have irregular periods, which means the time between their periods varies and it is hard to know when their next period is due.

When you first start having periods they might be irregular for a few months and then become regular, or they might remain irregular. Most women learn to know when their period is coming.

How long will it last?

It can take anything from 2 to 8 days for all the built-up lining of the uterus to dribble out. Some girls have short periods, others have longer ones. Sometimes it varies from one period to the next.

How much blood will there be?

Only about 1 to 6 tablespoons of blood and tissue comes out, although it may look and feel like more.

Do you have periods for the rest of your life?

Having periods is a sign that you are able to have a baby. A woman stops having periods gradually when she is in her 40s or 50s. This is called her menopause.

Catching the Flow

You need to use something to collect the blood and tissue as it comes out of your vagina, otherwise it will seep into your clothes. Your great-grandmother probably used strips of cloth, which she had to wash out and use again. These days you can buy special products to use.

Pads

Pads are made of layers of soft cotton or other material, which soak up the blood. They are held in place with a sticky strip that attaches the pad to your underpants. It is a good idea to try different sized pads out to see which sort you prefer.

You will be able to see when your pad needs changing, usually several times a day. Because the blood is exposed to the air, pads can develop a slight smell and you might feel more comfortable with a fresh one, and it's more hygienic, too.

When you've used a pad you can wrap it up in toilet paper, or put it in a plastic or paper bag, and put it in the trash can. Don't flush it down the toilet because it can easily block up the whole system.

Tampons

A tampon is made of very absorbent cotton rolled up into a small cylinder shape and it fits right inside your vagina. It has a string attached to the bottom so you can pull it out again easily. Some kinds have a cardboard or plastic tube on the outside which helps you put it in place or, with others, you can just use your fingers. The box you buy the tampons in will have a set of helpful instructions and diagrams in it.

When you put a tampon in, remember that your vagina tips up and backwards so you will have to put it in at the same angle. You might find it difficult to put in the first time, but if you relax and try again, you will soon find it quite easy. You will know if it is in properly because it will feel comfortable. You can't 'lose' a tampon inside you because your cervix stops it from going farther than your vagina.

There are several different sizes of tampons to soak up different amounts of blood. Sometimes, if your flow is really heavy, you might choose to wear a tampon and a pad.

It is not so easy to tell when your tampon needs changing, but it is important that you do this at least every four hours. Wear a pad overnight.

Washing your hands before and after you change your tampon is important to prevent any risk of infection getting into your vagina.

Tampons can be flushed down the toilet or wrapped up and put in the trash can.

Which is best for me?

Different things suit different people. You can try out pads and tampons and see which you like better.

Being prepared

It's a good idea to keep a supply of pads or tampons at home all the time and to carry a spare with you if you have your period, or think it might be coming. However, if your period comes and you don't have one, there are things you can use in the meantime. Anything you can use as a pad to soak up the blood will do, such as rolled-up toilet paper, a handkerchief or tissues, etc. You can always ask a teacher, or another girl or woman to help you.

More About Your Menstrual Cycle

Period pains

Some girls and women get cramps just before or during their periods. These feel like a dull or a very strong ache in the lower abdomen. There are things you can do to relieve this pain, like warming your tummy or lower back with a heating pad, taking a hot bath or doing gentle exercise.

Other secretions

Between your periods you may notice other secretions from your vagina. Depending on the time of your cycle they may look white, thick and tacky, white and runny, or like clear egg white. Some girls have a lot, and some not very much. They have a smell of their own, and this is perfectly natural. If it seems unusual, check it out with your doctor.

Feelings

Just before your period comes (and sometimes during it) you may feel tired or irritable or very emotional. You might have a craving for certain kinds of foods, find you can't concentrate on things, or want to be left alone.

These are all perfectly natural feelings and you might learn to recognize some of them as signs that your period is getting close. Telling other people around you can help them to be more understanding.

Your first period

If you have absolutely no idea what is happening to you, your first period can take you by surprise. You can talk to your mother, older sister, or someone you trust about having periods.

When your first period starts you might not feel ready for it. That's OK. You don't have to change a single thing about the way you are, just because you've started having periods. They may seem like a hassle at first, but, like with anything new, you will find that you get used to them very quickly.

Having your period is a sign that you have become a young woman. It is something to feel proud of.

...AND NOW. I'M AFRAID I'M GONNA HAVE TO BE a **GIRL** AND NOT BE ALLOWED TO GALLOP ABOUT ANYMORE AND NOT WIN THE DERBY **EVER** AND...

BUT, HORSE DEAR... YOU CAN BE A HORSE JUST AS **LONG** AS YOU **LIKE**! THE BEST HORSE THERE IS! AND IF YOU SHOULD EVER DECIDE TO BE A GIRL INSTEAD... WHY, I BET YOU'D WIN THE DERBY. **ANYWAY**!!

I LOVE YOU, GRAM! I WISH YOU WERE **MY GRANDMA**, TOO...

WELL, YOU KNOW, MY **FATHER** WAS A PALAMINO STALLION UNTIL HE WAS FIFTEEN... THAT MUST MAKE US **FAMILY**, YOU AND I...

I THINK I JUST TALKED MYSELF INTO A VERY **WEIRD** GRANDCHILD!...

GALLOP GALLOP

GALLOP

37

Boys: Maturing Sexually

Puberty begins for a boy any time after you are about nine. Your penis and testicles start to grow bigger, and at about the time you start to grow pubic hair you also begin to make sperm inside your testicles. From your testicles the sperm moves into the epididymis, where they mature. They then move through two sperm tubes called the vas deferens to the seminal vesicles, where they are stored, together with a special fluid called seminal fluid, which keeps the sperm alive and active.

The sperm and seminal fluid (together called semen) can come out of your penis at the times when you have an erection. This is called an **ejaculation**.

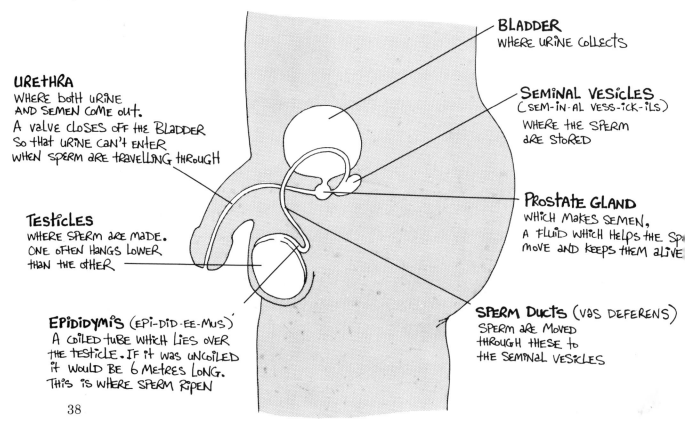

BLADDER
WHERE URINE COLLECTS

SEMINAL VESICLES
(SEM-IN-AL VESS-ICK-ILS)
WHERE THE SPERM
ARE STORED

PROSTATE GLAND
WHICH MAKES SEMEN,
A FLUID WHICH HELPS THE SP
MOVE AND KEEPS THEM ALIVE

SPERM DUCTS (VAS DEFERENS)
SPERM ARE MOVED
THROUGH THESE TO
THE SEMINAL VESICLES

URETHRA
WHERE both URINE
AND SEMEN COME out.
A valve CLOSES OFF the BLADDER
So that URINE CAN'T ENTER
WHEN SPERM are travelling through

TESTICLES
WHERE SPERM are made.
ONE often HANGS LOWER
than the other

EPIDIDYMIS (EPI-DID-EE-MUS)
A coiled tube which LIES OVER
the testicle. IF it was UNCOILED
it would BE 6 METRES LONG.
THIS is where SPERM RIPEN

38

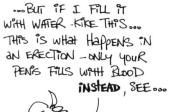

Erections

You have probably had erections from time to time, ever since you were a baby. Your penis becomes bigger and harder and stands up from your body. Blood fills the spongy tissue in your penis and it is held there by the tightening of special muscles in the base of your penis.

You can get an erection at all sorts of times:
— when your penis has been rubbing up against something;
— when you are feeling warm, sensual and sexy in bed (often when you wake up in the morning);
— when you are having sexy thoughts, feelings or dreams;
— when you've been touching or rubbing your penis because it feels nice. This is called **masturbation**.

During puberty you can get an erection at unexpected times — in church, in class, riding in the car, on the bus or at the beach. This can make you feel self-conscious or worried that someone will notice. Lots of boys find ways of hiding it: with a jacket, a towel or a book, or perhaps by sitting in a different way. It usually goes away after a few minutes.

What makes your penis go limp again?

You can't make an erection go away. Your penis will go limp again when your sexy feelings pass, when you stop thinking about it, or when you masturbate and have an orgasm.

Ejaculations

An ejaculation is when muscles around your seminal vesicles (where sperm is stored) squeeze out semen. During an orgasm these muscles contract and squirt semen out; at other times when you get excited the semen may be squeezed out more slowly and just leak out of your penis.

You can have an ejaculation when you have been masturbating and have an orgasm or you might have your first ejaculation when you are asleep. You may have been dreaming about something exciting and wake up to find whitish fluid on yourself, your pajamas and your sheets. There is only a small amount, but it feels cold and wet. This is called a 'wet dream.'

Although only about a teaspoonful of semen comes out, it contains about 400 million sperm! This is a sign that you are physically capable of fathering a child.

How often do boys have wet dreams?

Everyone is different. Some boys hardly ever have them; others have them a few times a week.

What's it like the first time you ejaculate?

It's like anything that's new; you can feel a mixture of things — excited, pleased, curious, confused, or nothing much at all. Whatever you feel you can be sure that an ejaculation is just a natural and healthy sign that you are growing up.

Some myths

Some boys have been made to think that if they don't do something about their erect penis to make it go down again, it will be damaged. This isn't true. There are a lot of other myths about boys' penises.

You can't make your penis grow bigger by masturbating, nor will it drop off if you do it 250 times. The size of your penis is also not important sexually.

Sexual Feelings and Orgasms

When men and women, girls and boys feel sensual, they often feel warm and good all over their bodies. When they have sexual feelings they often feel warm and tingly and excited, especially around their genitals.

Sensual and sexual feelings can start and then just fade away. Sometimes they become stronger and there is a build-up of very pleasurable and intense feelings, especially around the genitals, until the person feels a sudden rush of excitement and warm feelings spread all through the body in big waves. This is called an orgasm, and it leaves you feeling relaxed and peaceful and happy.

Some people say that orgasms feel like:
— whooshing down a big slide;
— being lost in space;
— being washed over by a big wave of pleasure.

Some people have orgasms from the time they are little, although as they get older they usually feel stronger and are more intense and therefore more pleasurable.

One of the ways people can give themselves sexual feelings or an orgasm is from rubbing or stroking parts of their bodies. You might discover that it feels nice to stroke or rub your penis, if you are a boy, or around your clitoris if you are a girl. This is called masturbating.

Masturbation is not harmful, but feeling guilty or worried or frightened about doing it can be. Some people masturbate often; some people, hardly ever.

43

Your Body and Other People

It's good to feel happy and natural and unembarassed about your body. It's also perfectly OK to have times when you want to have some privacy and you would prefer other people to keep out when you are changing, or taking a bath, for instance. It's your body and your right to decide who can see it and who can't.

The same goes for letting other people touch your body. Being cuddled, kissed, tickled or touched can give us all sorts of feelings.

Good touching makes you feel good.

Bad touching makes you feel bad — uncomfortable, annoyed, uneasy, nervous or ashamed. You have a right to say no to bad touching.

If someone touches you in a way that feels bad or confusing, or tries to make you do things you don't want to do, you are right to tell them to stop, even if it is someone you know and like. If the person won't stop, or tries to do it again later, then it's a good idea to tell an adult you trust and who will listen to you.

Good secrets, bad secrets

Some people like touching kids in a bad or confusing way but they know they will get into trouble if anyone finds out. So they try to make kids keep it secret, by threatening them with trouble if they tell, or by tricking them into making a promise not to tell.

There is a difference between a secret that feels good and a secret that feels bad.

Good secrets, like a surprise birthday party for your mom or dad, don't stay secret for long and they feel good.

Bad secrets stay secret and feel bad. It's important to tell an adult you trust if anyone tries to make you keep a bad secret.

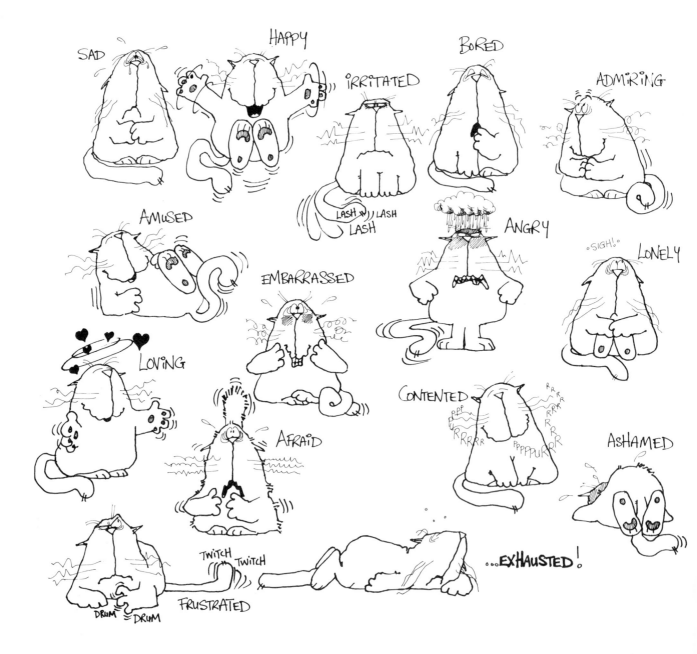

You and Your Feelings

About Your Feelings

A feeling is your body and mind responding to something that is happening to you. When we say we are feeling hungry or cold or tired we are talking about sensations. When we say we are feeling sad or angry or lonely we are talking about emotions. The sorts of feelings we are talking about in this chapter are **emotions**.

We are all able to feel lots of different emotions. Munchkin (opposite) is showing just some of them.

Feelings can have a big effect on you.

They can make you want to laugh, shout, cry or curl up by yourself. Learning to understand your emotions is important. It is like knowing you need to rest when you are tired, eating when you are hungry or putting on warm clothes when you are cold.

Sometimes it is difficult to figure out why you have a feeling.

Sometimes it is easy to know why you have a feeling and sometimes it's hard. You might be feeling very grumpy one evening and not know why. The reason only becomes obvious later. You realize that all evening your parents were fussing over your younger brother and ignoring you.

There is always a reason for having a feeling.

It is important to remember that just because you can't always figure out why you feel something it doesn't mean there isn't a reason for it.

Always pay attention to your feelings.

Sometimes it is difficult to know whether to pay attention to a feeling or not. You might have good feelings about a friend because he is a lot of fun to be with, but for some reason you feel you can't quite trust him. (Later you find he has been talking about you behind your back.)

Feelings Help You in Lots of Ways

Your feelings let you know what's good for you.

Your feelings let you know what's bad for you.

It's important to pay attention to feelings that tell you something isn't right. For instance, feeling scared, suspicious, anxious or uncomfortable about someone or some-thing usually makes you want to get away. So it's a good idea to do just that. Your feelings are like your own personal radar, so it pays to listen to what they are telling you, even if you aren't sure why.

Your feelings can help you sort things out.

Your feelings can help you solve problems and make decisions if you learn to pay attention to them. Often, when you find out the facts, you will realize that you were right to listen to your feelings.

Using your imagination and your feelings together

Your brain can create pictures, situations and conversations—this is called your imagination.

Imagining (or dreaming) something can give you the same feelings you would have if it were real. This means you can use your imagination to experience things without actually doing anything. Paying attention to the feelings you have when you use your imagination can help you make decisions.

You can use your imagination...

... to work out what you could do if a real problem came up. For example:

What if I was at the movies with my friends and I lost them in the crowd?
— I could freak out.
— I could go to the bus stop and wait for them there. But what if they don't go there straight away?
— I could wait outside the theater and look for them. But I might miss them in the crowd.
— We could make an arrangement about what to do if one of us gets lost. Yes, that feels best.

... to practice saying something to someone so that it will be easier when it comes to actually doing it. For example:

I want to ask Mom what it feels like to have sex.
I feel embarrassed about asking her.
I'll practice saying it.
'Mom, what's it like having sex?'
No, that's not right. How embarrassing!
'Mom, I feel embarrassed about asking you this, but what's it like having sex?'
That feels better. I'll try it.

... to make you feel good about yourself.

Letting Your Feelings Out Is Good for You

Letting your feelings out is a way of unloading the stresses and strains of things that are affecting you badly. For instance, if something is making you really angry you could try going off by yourself and shouting, thumping a cushion, writing down your angry feelings, painting a big angry picture, or finding someone you trust and talking to them about it.

Even when there are situations where you can't show how you feel, it's still important to find an opportunity to let your built-up feelings out. For instance, if some kids at school are mean to you and make you feel like crying but you don't want them to see, then it's good to get away somewhere so you can have a good cry.

The stresses from storing up your feelings all the time can actually make you physically ill. Bottled-up feelings can also make life difficult for you and others. They may come spilling out at the wrong time or be directed at the wrong person.

It can be hard to show how you feel.

It's all very well saying that it's good for you to show your feelings, but sometimes this can be hard to do, especially at times when other people don't accept how you feel, or say something that makes you feel worse than you already do.

People behave like this because:
— they have been taught that their own feelings are not OK and they treat other people the same way;
— they are frightened of their own and other people's feelings.

Another reason why it can be hard to show your feelings is because girls and boys and men and women are often expected to behave in certain ways. In our society many people think it is OK for boys to show their angry or tough feelings but not OK to show their sad, vulnerable, tender or caring feelings.

On the other hand, it is often OK for girls to show their sad, caring and gentle sides, but not so OK to show their angry, tough or adventurous feelings.

Girls and boys, men and women are all people and all have the same sorts of feelings. Letting out your 'acceptable' feelings and holding in your 'unacceptable' feelings will be bad for you in the long run.

Unfortunately, a lot of people decide to hide their feelings because they find it hard to show them and don't know what else to do. They do this in different ways.

54

Sometimes if you share your feelings with others you will be surprised to find that they feel pretty much like you!

Taking Care of Your Feelings

Just as there are ways of taking care of your body, so there are ways of taking care of your feelings. Learning to do this is important if you want to feel strong.

It's important to act on your feelings.

There are all sorts of times when people ask you to do things you don't want to do that are perfectly fair — like being asked to dry the dishes or to tidy up your room. There are other times when you have the right to say no if you don't want to do something.

Saying no isn't always easy, especially if you are worried that the other person won't like you if you say no, and you are being pressured into saying yes.

Practice makes it easier to say no.

If you practice saying no to little things you will find it easier to say no when it is really important.

How you say no is important too. If you say it clearly and firmly, it helps. Sometimes it also helps to say how you feel — this makes it clear why you don't want to do something.

If you say yes when you really don't want to do something then you probably won't enjoy yourself. You are likely to end up feeling anxious, grumpy or resentful.

It takes time and practice to stand up for how you feel.

Here are some basic rules:
1. Feelings are real, not imaginary.
2. There is always a reason for how you feel.
3. Following your feelings when you make decisions is always best for you in the end.

Changing Feelings and Thoughts

During puberty boys and girls think about lots of new things and feel lots of new feelings.

— You may feel more emotional, up and down.
— You may feel like being on your own more often.
— You may feel awkward and clumsy.
— You may become more attracted to other boys and girls in a different way from before.
— You may start to have heroes and heroines, older people you really admire and try to copy.
— You may feel like dressing like older kids do.
— You may feel less interested in younger kids' games and want to spend time with older kids.
— You may feel like being more independent.
— You may find it is harder to get along with your parents.

All these things are a usual part of growing up.

You and Other People

You can have all sorts of feelings about other people, those you don't know, as well as those you do know. These feelings can be bad feelings, the ones you have when you resent, fear, distrust or dislike someone. Or they can be good feelings, the ones you have when you like, admire, trust, enjoy or love someone.

The People You Live With

The people you live with affect your feelings a lot because you spend a lot of time with them. Generally people who live together are called a family. There are all kinds of different ways in which people can choose to live together. For instance:

Joanna and her daughters Michelle and
    Megan
Harry and his son and daughter Daniel and
    Chloe
Grandfather Li, Grandmother Soo, mother,
    father and three children
Polly and David and their four children

Deborah and Paul
Sharon and Cyrene and Anna
David and Brian
Richard and his daughter Simone, and
    Helen and her son Abe
Dan and Mary and her sons Joe and Josh

Problems

Families can have a lot of good times together. But when any group of people lives together there can be arguments, disagreements and resentments at times.

Problem solving

Getting along well with the people you live with doesn't mean pretending everything is fine by hiding your feelings. There's nothing wrong with having bad feelings caused by differences between people, it's what you do with them that counts.

Here are ideas to help people sort problems out:

1. Choose a time when there won't be any interruptions.
2. State the situation.
3. Say how you feel about it.
4. Ask for what you want done about it.
5. Be prepared to be reasonable because sometimes a compromise will be necessary.

Sometimes things don't run smoothly and sometimes you might not get what you want. At the very least, talking about problems can clear away the build-up of resentments between people and help make things easier.

60

Friends

There are all sorts of reasons why you choose a person as a friend.

'My brother is my friend; he helps me with my schoolwork.'

'My mom is my friend; she's kind to me.'
'Stevie and Munchkin are my friends; we do fun things together.'
'Icecream is my friend. Sometimes that kid is really smart.'

61

Friends are especially important. You can talk to some friends for hours on end and never run out of things to say. Even though you may have occasional fights or feel that you want to be by yourself for a while, a friend is usually someone you want to spend time with.

A good friendship is an equal friendship:
— you decide together about what you want to do;
— you give and take and share equally;
— you can trust each other;
— you are honest with each other;
— you both make an effort to sort out any problems you have together;
— you can count on one another in the good times and the bad times;
— you both have other friends too.

FORGET IT —
HE's FOUND DIAL-A-JOKE
AGAIN...
THE PHONE'LL BE
TIED UP FOR HOURS...

Being your own friend

Most people have times in their lives when they feel lonely because they haven't any friends. Whether you have friends or not, you can always be a friend to yourself — read a book, go to the movies, make something, play a game on your own, write a letter to someone you know. You could also tell someone in your family how you are feeling. Just talking about things can make a difference. Sometimes someone else may have a helpful suggestion.

Making friends

Some people find it easy to make friends and some people find it hard.

It's easier if:
— you have interests in common;
— you are introduced by another friend:
— you know they like you too.

It's harder if:
— you feel shy;
— you feel you aren't welcome;
— the other person belongs to a group you're not part of;
— you're new to your neighborhood or school and you don't know anyone.

If you feel you want to be friends with someone, why not go up to them and ask them? You may find they've been wanting to do the same thing. Another good idea is to join a club or try out for a sports team. There will be other people there with the same interests as you, which is always a good place to start. Remember, if everyone waited for others to make friends with them, nothing would happen.

Changes in friendships

You won't always feel the same way about your friends and they won't always feel the same about you. Friendships change all the time, especially when you are growing and changing yourself.

You may find that your friend suddenly wants to do new things that you don't feel ready to try just yet, or she or he starts hanging round a new crowd of people you don't really like. Or your friend might want to keep on doing the same old things that you're just not interested in any more. Some friendships just drift apart without either of you really noticing, but sometimes the break-up can be painful.

'Jody and I were friends for ages, then she started avoiding me. She never said why and now I'm starting to worry that other people won't go on liking me. Besides, I really miss her.'

Attraction

As part of puberty you can also find yourself feeling strongly attracted to another person, wanting to be near them and thinking about them a lot. It may be someone of the same sex or of the other sex. It may be someone you know well or don't know very well at all. You may want to let this person know how you feel by telling him or her, writing a note, or even by using mental telepathy! You may decide you don't want to do anything about these feelings and that's OK too.

- There might be someone special you really like but not know what to do about it.
- You might feel under a lot of pressure to get a girlfriend or a boyfriend when you don't really want one.
- You might worry about feeling left out if you don't have one.
- You might feel unattractive and worry a lot about being too fat or too awkward or too pimply and think you're never going to attract anyone.

It's important to remember that the things that make a person a good friend still count. It is easy to fall for the 'popular' people, but just because they are popular doesn't necessarily mean they're right for you. And having a new interest in someone else doesn't mean you have to forget your old friends.

Above all, follow your own feelings and be around people who make you feel comfortable and who like you just as you are.

It's OK to Be You!

Now that you are on your way to growing up, how does it feel and what will it mean?

'Making my own mind up about things.'
'Taking responsibility for myself.'
'Being who I want to be.'

If things get confusing it helps to remember:

— that whatever you feel, there are others who probably feel the same as you do;
— you can go at your own pace;
— you don't have to do or be anything just because others expect you to;
— it can help a lot to talk about it with someone you trust;
— It's OK to be you!

69

70